A Vampire's Story

By C. E. Metcalf

Chapter 1

The year was 1895 I was young man the age of twenty-four. Back then I was full of energy with big dreams. How someday I was going to be rich. If I had only known what I know now. I have experienced things that very few would understand.

I was walking home one night from a night on the town. I had already walked my lover home. The weather was still warm for a fall evening. It was an incredibly quiet and peaceful walk. Normally it would take me about a have hour to get home. But for some reason I decided to take a unique way. To this day I don't know why. All I remember was I had this strange feeling someone was calling me there. In the distance I saw a man standing alongside of the road. At first it seemed quite odd. He was tall and thin and was dressed in a style of clothes I had never seen before. I see you have found your way he said. Why do you say that I asked? Because I summoned you here. If you don't believe me, try, and walk away. I Laughed aloud and shook my head. OK I'll bite what's the catch? There is no catch just a deal you made with me a few years ago. Remember when you almost drown. You wanted God to save you, but he didn't when you went under for the last time, you cried out Devil save me. And I did. Remember when you woke up on the beach a man was standing beside you. And when you blinked your eyes, he disappeared. He told you he would return someday. Today is you lucky day I am here. I thought for a moment and said you don't even look like him. How can you be the devil? I can take many forms the stranger said. Everyone has a little Devil inside them. OK Devil what do you what with me. Only your soul the devil said. But I am willing to make you a deal. And what kind of a deal is that I asked? I will make you immortal and exchange for your soul. Being immortal, you can never die. You will always look like you do now and never grow old. I will never grow old I said. Know the devil said. You will look just like you do now forever. Wow I thought to me. All kinds of ideas were going through my mind. Could this be real I said to myself. Or is my mind playing tricks on me. Without moving his lips. This is the only chance you have. The devil said. I also know the Doctor said you have an enlarged heart. You're a heart attack waiting to happen. How did you know? I know everything about you. The Devil said with a laugh. You just need to sign here. You can use my back to write on if you like. He gently pulled a contract from his back pocket. When he unfolded it. It was about ten pages long. What is all this? I asked. It's nothing to be concerned about. Just stuff to make it legal. You can just read it later. Being young I didn't know any better I signed my name. The devil laughed aloud. One thing I forgot to tell you. To be an immortal. I had to make you a vampire. What are you talking about? Vampires aren't real. But they are the devil said. With a loud laugh he disappeared into the night. I stood there alone in silence wondering what to do next. A strange feeling came over me. A cold chill came up my spine. I could feel my heart beating in my chest. The beats were getting further apart. My heart was slowing down with every beat. Am I going to die, I asked him? The Devil laughed and said everyone must die. As my heart slowed down so did my breathing. My legs were getting weak.

I could feel myself slowly falling to the ground. When I awoke confusion came over me. I tried to sit up and could not. My head hit something solid. I put my hand in front of my face, And I started to scream. I knew then I was buried alive. There was no air going in or out of my lungs. I began laughing. Then I remembered the deal with the Devil. He made me immortal. But how do I get out of this coffin? With little effort I pushed the lid open and the dirt above me flew away like dust in the wind. And like magic I raised myself to the ground above.

I stood there in the darkness looking down at my grave. Without a second thought I turned my back to it and walked away into the night. Not knowing where I was going. A magnet was pulling me It was a strength stronger than my own. I tried to change direction but couldn't. I could see a vision in my head. It was one of a young Girl sitting alone on a bench. With what seemed like a blink of an eye I was standing behind her. I could already taste the blood in her vanes. I wanted to pull myself back. What I was about to do I knew was wrong. I reached around her head I put my hand over her mouth and twisted her head. I could feel her neck break. It sounded like I broke a stick in half. The

blood started to spray from the main artery.
Like a crazed animal I drank it as fast as I could.
The more I drank of the red warm liquid the
more I wanted. Her body lay limb on the grassy
ground in front of me. I had no feeling or
remorse about the murder I just did. I could see
the sun starting to rise in the distance. My body
was starting to feel warm, almost hot. The
sunlight was causing my body to burn. I could
see the smoke starting to rise from my hands.
Without realizing what I did somehow, I got
myself to a dark cold room. My vision was like
that of a cat. There was only one thing in the
room. There was an old coffin standing up in
the corner. I slowly picked it up and laid it flat
on the floor. I stood there and looked at it for
what seemed like a long time. I opened the lid
with a wave of my hand I brushed away the
years of dusk and cobwebs. Just like I had done
it a hundred times before. And then I laid down
in it and shut the lid. I laid there in silence for a
moment. And my thought's drifted away. And
there was nothing. Nothing put silence. I could
not even hear my heartbeat. Because I didn't
have one. For the reason I am one of the living
dead. I only come out at night when the rest of
the world is sleeping. The nights became

months and the months become years. And
then I had no sense of time. The years go by like
hours. And the blood trail I leave behind gets
longer.

Chapter 2

A century has gone by, and I don't look a day
older. The year is 1995 many things have
changed in the world except me. I still look at
my hands and they are of a young man. I have
no reflection in a mirror or otherwise. I have
survived the many years by the thirst for blood.
Sometimes I have killed animals as little as a rat.
To quench my thirst. And when the opportunity
arose a late -night wanderer. The many lives I
have taken without a second thought. I have
learned to blend in with the changing of time. I
have changed my identity more times that I can
remember. I have learned to dress the same as
modern people. I must fit in quite well because
other people don't notice. For a man that died
One Hundred years ago I live quit well. I have a
private home across town that I acquired in one
of many Businesses deals I have made. When
the sun starts to come up- I lock myself in my

basement and lie in my coffin until dust. Quite often I have thought about being a day walker once again. But I knew it would never be possible. The devil's crooked deal cursed me into roaming this world threw eternity. Many time's people have tried to kill me and all I do is laugh and they become my victim and their warm blood becomes mine. I want no one to pity me. The crimes I have committed I deserve the curse I carry. And only the return of my soul will take it away. I search the world trying to find redemption. To right my many wrongs. Every night I commit more. It is now a cool October evening the sun just went down, and the darkness came over the world again. I open the lid of my coffin and standing in front of me was the one man I didn't want to see. He looked at me with those eyes of fire. The man that put me here the devil. I flew from my resting place and grabbed him by the throat and tried to sink my blood thirsty fangs into his neck. My jaws clenched shut like that of a wild dog. And found nothing. There was no blood. The devil hit me in the chest with the palm of his hand and I flew backwards landing on my back. With a voice as loud as thunder he said you cannot kill me. You can't beat me no matter how hard you try. Just like you I will always be hear. I created you in my image. All these years you thought you were alone on this world. I had you fooled he said with a sneer. I have been here. Long before you were turned. Long before this world was formed. Way before the world was created God and I were rivals. God is good and I am evil. God created the heavens and the earth. And he created Adam & Eve. He turned me into the serpent I was doomed to crawl on my belly threw the world forever. What he didn't realize when Eve sinned and took a bite of an apple from the tree of life. I was able to turn back to my natural form pure evil. And I started the battle of good and evil. Through the minds of others, I control the evil throughout the world. What did you do create me to help you with your dirty work? As I screamed the hatred for him grew worse. I can see your angry with me the Devil said, I like it. The madder you get the more out of control you become. I can smell your thirst for blood. Your craven is getting stronger by the hour. Eventually, you will have to drink again. If only I could drink with you. I have no thirst. I have no hunger I just have your thoughts. The madness and your animal instinct for survival. I looked him straight

in the eyes and said. Some night I will find a way
to kill you. I hope you do the devil said as he
faded away into the night. The anger was
burning in me like a hot fire. I picked up my
coffin with one hand and through it across the
room. Smashing it against the wall. The night
was dark and gloomy my thirst was still growing.
And only blood would satisfy it. I could hear a
church bell ringing in the distance. I knew that
churches were holy ground. But I could not
enter in on my own. I would have to be invited
by someone. When invited the curse is
temporarily lifted. And I am human for a short
while. The longer I am on holy ground the more
I start to age. Within a short -time I turn into an
old man. As soon as I step off holy ground my
early age returns. Once the Congregation
thought I dropped dead because of my age.
They did not feel a Heartbeat. And they buried
me in a shallow grave. And that night I returned
scaring them to death. I then left the building
and waited for them to exit. And one by one
they became my victim. When I was done there
were twenty bodies lying in the church yard.
Their faces had all turned white because of their
blood being drank.

I had filled my thirst temporarily and I knew it

was time to move on. Since I smashed my coffin
into splinter's I had to find a new resting place. I
knew my welcome had run out in this town. I
could hear the town-folks screaming as they
were putting together a search party for me.
Will they ever learn? They know they cannot kill
me. Even if I were captured breaking away
would be easy. With a quick twist of my body, I
disappeared into the night. If seemed like only
minutes had went by and I found myself in a
whole different town many miles away. It was a
big city that I did not recognize. There were
streetlights on every street. I found a
newspaper box. Smashing the door open with
my fist I pulled out a paper. The date on it was
April 2nd 1 9 9 7. I had jumped ahead in time
about two years. All the years I have bounced
through time I really have no idea how I do it. It
must be magic of some kind. I subconsciously
learned to use. It's only happens when the odds
are against me. I knew the sun would be coming
up soon and I had to find a safe- haven until
dusk. A vision flashed into my head of and old
run-down building not far away. A second later I
was standing in front of it. It was exceptionally
large and made of stone. I entered through the
front door and found piles of rubbish all around

the room. In the center of the room stood a large machine of some kind. With a quick observation I soon came to a realize this place was once a factory. I started opening doors and found a staircase that went to the basement. I could smell the cold dampness of earth. I knew then it had a dirt floor. After walking down, a dozen steps I was standing on the cold earth one again. There was only an empty room with no windows. I waved my hand and my coffin appeared in front of me. With a wave of my other hand my grave appeared. I placed my coffin into the six- foot hole. When it hit the solid ground, the lid slowly opened. As I laid my body down once again the lid closed and the earth filled in above me. The moon was full and bright and filled the night sky. After waking up from my resting place my thirst for blood was overwhelming me once again. It controlled me like an addiction. The more I drank of the warm red liquid the more I wanted. If only I had a continuous supply. I would be insanely happy. Said the words of a madman. It is hard to be a madman if you are not a man. I am an animal in a man's form. I have no heart only the instinct for survival. I knew I had to drink and soon.

As I walked the City street's I hid myself in the

shadows patiently waiting for my next victim to appear. It was a warm spring night. The streets were full of people. All the businesses were open. Far away I could hear music playing from some establishment. There is so many possibilities to choose from. From children to old adults. Thought my animal mind. I sat on a rooftop looking down, patiently waiting for the right time to feed again. The evening was getting late the crowds were starting to thin. Up the street I could see a lonely shopper. With a large bag in both arms. I could smell his sweat from the heavy load he was carrying. Every step he took seemed to be harder & harder. He finally sat down on a sidewalk bench to rest. Sitting his bag beside him he closed his eyes to catch his breath. I took a quick look around and saw no one else on the street. I jumped from the rooftop and landed quietly behind him. I put my hand over his mouth to muffle his scream. But there was none. How lucky can I get the man had just died of a heart attack. I knew his blood was still warm. I sank my fangs into his neck and sucked his blood as if sucking threw a straw.

When I was done his face was as pale as a ghost. I laid his limp body on the ground and disappeared into the darkness.

The darkness. O' Yes the darkness my welcome friend. The only friend I have. The darkness has always been there for me. My only home. If only I could walk in the sunlight and feel the heat on my face once again.

Dawn was starting to come over the arisen. My shell of a body started to smoke. Flames were flying from my fingertips. I quickly transported myself back to the old building I was at the night before.

With a wave of my other hand my coffin appeared in front of me. I laid down once again and my mind drifted off into emptiness.

I was awakened from my resting place with the shaking of the ground. The earth around me moved like I have never felt before. I flew out of my coffin faster than a beam of light. I stood in the shadows outside the building watching. There was a large machine of some sort knocking down the building. In the matter of an hour, it was leveled to the ground. How dare they? I asked myself. The anger was starting to boil inside of me. I felt rage like I had never felt before. There stood seven men around what was left of the large structure. I started walking from the shadows towards them. One of them saw me coming remarked who the hell are you. They could see the anger in my eyes. I grabbed him by the chin and threw him over top the machine breaking his back as he hit the ground.

Two more came at me. I hit them both in the chest with the palm of each hand. Knocking them to the ground. The fourth removed a pistol from the back of his jacket. Firing twice two bullets directly in the center of my chest. As I stood there laughing the bullets pushed out of my body. The man froze in terror as the bullet holes healed themselves. The others took off running like scared little children.

I knew then the night would be difficult. Just like many times before the law would be putting together a search party to find me.

I laugh at the law. No law has ever stopped me. Laws are for humans. Human I am not. I know I am a monster in the form of a man. Which man? I look nothing like any man I have ever encountered. My hair is dark, but my skin is pale. Like that of a dead man. When I drink my skin turns to a normal the color of the age I once was. I was Twenty- Four years of age when I was turned into a vampire. So many years ago. So carefree and young. I have wondered about it many times. Being a young lad again without a worry in the world. Not knowing what the future has in store.

I know what my future brings. Night after night of hunting for my next prey. The drinking of some wanderer's blood. The insanity and madness of a thirst I can never totally quench. I am nothing but a blood thirsty animal. Nothing more nothing less.

There must be another way. All I want is a never -ending supply of blood. Only a madman would want that.

I picked up one of the bodies I had left on the ground. And I quickly drank. At once a warm burst of life come threw me. A surge of power and strength. That only another immortal would feel. I asked myself more than once if I was the only one of my kind. Am I doomed? To roam this world alone. If only I had someone by my side. Someone as blood graved as me.

With a twist of my body, I vanished into the night bringing myself to another time and place. Searching again to shelter myself from the sun's rays.

I found myself walking in the woods. Near to me I could here to sounds of the night creatures looking for food. In my mind I could see a lonely fawn feeding on the grass.

It had been a long time since I drank the blood of an animal. I jumped on its back bringing it to the ground. With a twist of its neck, it broke like a stick. Blood started to spray from the main artery like a fountain. The taste of it was gamy but vampires can't be picky. I drank my fill and tossed the limp body into the underbrush that was close by.

As I stood there wiping the blood from around my lip's I had a vision of a cemetery. It looked as if It hadn't been used in years. I quickly transported myself there.

Off in one corner stood a stone building. By the

structure I knew it was a mausoleum. it was
sealed with a large steel door. Perfect I said to
myself. I grabbed a hold of the old rusty padlock
and twisted it off. It fell to the ground with the
sound of a small pebble. When I pulled it open
there was a creek from the rusty metal. I then
walked inside to the age-old smell of death. It
made me feel right at home.

As always, I waved my hand and my coffin
appeared and I laid myself down to rest.

When I woke the day was just turning dusk. The
sun was settling in the distance. As I walked out
of my stone resting place. The evening air was
cool but still. The old cemetery was as quite as a
tomb. Not even a breeze in the air. Far in the
distance I could hear the slight rubble of
thunder. A stormy might be headed this way.

One step at a time I slowly walked down what
was once a driveway. At the end of it was what
seemed like a seasonal road. Which was not
very well maintained. Every few feet I found
large pot- holes in the road. This was the road

to nowhere I thought to myself. My thirst for blood was starting to form in my mouth. I knew I had to drink soon. As I walked a strange feeling came over me. Like I was being watched. But by who? There was no one around. At least no one I could see. Then I remembered that feeling, the feeling of being alone. I have been alone every night for over years. Sometimes I wish I had a companion by my side just for the company. But on the other side of the coin, I would not want anyone to carry this curse. I prey on the living, drink their blood, and leave the drained body, from its normal color on the ground to rot. If only my shell of a body would rot and turn to dust. If only my existence would no longer be. But I knew it would never happen.

I just want to leave this dark hell that I exist in. I want this curse that I carry to the end.

As I walked down the road visions were flashing in an out of my head. Visions of my next victim. I could see a lonesome girl walking down a wooded path. Where to I had no idea. I longed for her warm blood to drink. The taste of her life being taken away as I drink. O yes, her blood. As I thought about it, I wanted it increasingly until I could no longer control the craving. Faster than the blink of an eye I transported myself near her. I stood in the shadows and waited for the right moment to strike. A sweet young girl. Why her? I asked myself. By then it was too late. I had already came up behind her and broke her neck like a pencil. As I held her dead body in my arms, I drained every warm ounce of her blood and dropped her to the ground like a broken doll. I knew by morning someone would find her. I had no remorse for what I had down. No remorse just like the others before her. If only I could be human again. And walk in the sun once again. I have thought many times about standing in the sun and let it burn and turn me to dust. But some on known power pulls me backwards. And this thirst oh yes, this thirst. The craving for blood from a dead human.

I haven't seen my own reflection in many years. I am just a creature of the night an animal like the other ones that roam the darkness. I have no friends no companion. On one hand I long for someone. But on the other I wouldn't what anyone else to have to carry this curse. The Vampires curse.

In a brief time, the dawn would soon be here once again. And I will lay myself in the stillness of my coffin. The one place where I feel safe. And my victims are safe from me. I will lay there like a corpse until the night comes once again.

I was back to my stone resting place. A place where the sun doesn't shine. A place that hadn't been entered until I showed up. For now, it will be my temporary home. A home where it is cool and damp and has the smell of death. O yes home sweet home.

As he entered the crypt, he coffin awaited him like a long-lost lover waiting for him to lay down. As he lay down a feeling of peace came over him as he shut the lid. And then there was silence the quietness of a tomb a temporary serenity until the darkness comes again.

Chapter 3

It seemed like my coffin lid just shut and it opened. I sat up once again having to face the night. I sat and listened to the silence of my tomb. There was nothing not even a breath. I don't even remember what it's like anymore. If only I could breathe in the coolness of the night air. As I removed myself from my coffee my thirst for blood was getting stronger. Who would my next victim be? Another lonely traveler.

As I stepped outside, I closed the door behind me. I stood there waiting like an animal waiting to attack. Then a vision came into my head. A young couple docking a rowboat. Where I did not know.

With the blink of an eye, I was there watching them from the shadows waiting for the right time. As I stood there watching my mouth craved for the taste of their blood. No one else was there but them. Faster than the speed of light I had come up behind them and broke their necks. They never had a chance. I stood there and held their bodies one in each hand sucking there blood from one neck to the other. When I was done, I picked them up one at a time and through them far into the lake into their watery grave. Where they will be lost forever.

My thirst has been filled for now. No, I need to blend in with the folks of my new home. With a wave of my hand, I transformed my clothing in a more modern look. From the outside I looked

like a typical businessman. Tonight, I choose to
be a lawyer. And I was planning to open a
practice here.

The city itself seemed quite busy. The shops
were open late. The people were still walking
back and forth going to different destinations. A
vampires dream I said to myself. Whatever a
dream may be. I heard some music planning
from a tavern close by that caught my interest,
so I headed there. The music was loud and
obnoxious and a lot different from my youth. A
few centuries have come and went since then.

As I got closer, I noticed a large man standing in
front of the door dressed in black leather. And
out front were vehicles that looked like large,
motorized bicycles. As I watched from the
shadows a man and woman came out of the
building and sat on one. As I watched them
closely the driver pushed a button and it roared
to life. The sound of it echoed the night air as
they rode away.

I tried to enter the establishment and the large
man stopped me. This place is for members
only and he pointed to the sign on the door.
Members only I said please tell me about this

place. What are you fucking stupid the man said? This place belongs to the Hell's Angels. I like the name I said. But I never realized there were Angels in hell. Are you trying to be a smart-ass he asked? I am quite smart I stated but I am not an ass. As ass is a for legged animal and I only have two. You are really starting to piss me off the large man said. You need to leave NOW he screamed. But I really don't want to leave I said. I would like to see the inside.

So, you want to see the inside he laughed. Very well I will take you inside you can go first. I know sooner opened the door and he kicked me in my back side pushing me to the floor. And know you have pissed me off I said. The crowd was laughing at my fall. Another big man came at me from the front and tried to grab me. But he got a surprise when I caught his hand and broke his wrist. As he screamed in pain the first big man came at me. I hit him in the chest with the palm of my hand pushing him across the room and up against the wall. This is getting to be fun I said as I laughed.

The next man came at me with a knife and at the speed of a blink I put it into his throat. Sending his dead body to the floor. Now the crowd was angry then out came the guns. I just held my ground as the bullets entered my body. AS fast as they hit my body was pushing them out and healing itself. The more they shot me the more I laughed. After I got bored with the bullets hitting me it was my turn. I started killing them one by one. When I finished there were almost twenty bodies all around the floor. A vampire's cuisine I drank the warm blood of people of different ages.

When I finished it was late into the night? The music was still playing as I shut the front door and left. My thirst was surely more than satisfied.

The sun would soon be coming up and I needed to return to my tomb. With my magic I transported myself close to the cemetery. Just as I expected no one was there. I opened the door of my tomb and turned around so I could watch the night sky. I could hear the howl of a wolf in the distance and the sounds of other night creatures moving about. In the distant east I could see the sun starting to rise. And the darkness was slowly turning to light. I could feel my skin starting to get warm from the morning light. Soon my skin would start to burn, and I would have to return to the solitude of my coffin.

As I woke up out of my nothingness, I could hear the thunder fill the sky. So, I closed my coffin and went outside. Lightning always interested me. It had a destructive force that no one could control. I tilted my head back and let the rain hit my face even though I could not feel it.

As I stood there my craving for blood was starting to take control of me again. I happen to notice a lost deer not too far from me. Animal blood is better than none I said to myself. Faster than the blink of an eye I was on its back forcing it to the ground. With a quick twist of its head, I broke its neck letting it die. I took my sharp fingernails and ripped the fur away from its neck so I could drink. Animal blood had that game e taste, but it served its purpose. A vampire can't be picky. When I was finished, I threw the dead body as far away as I could leaving it to rot. For now, my thirst has been met but only for now.

The lightning was cracking, and the thunder roared. And the rain itself is another story.

Some say it is God's way of cleansing the earth. Yes, but of what because evil still lurks in the darkness, I am proof of that. I am evil of the worse kind. I have no feeling no remorse just a never-ending thirst for blood. I am a Vampire a creature of the darkness. Someone that's only home is resting in the darkness of a coffin. I am of the living dead. A soul less shape in the shell of a man.

I noticed the rain run down my arms, but I did not feel it's cold. The clothes I wore were soaked but it did not bother me. I longed again for the blood of a human. Who would my next victim be? Somewhere in the darkness there is usually a late- night wanderer. Some poor soul just wandering about trying to produce a reason not to go home. Or a young lady on her way home. Or a hobo that no one will miss. Sometimes I can't help but wonder who missed me after they put me in the ground. Or the look on their faces when someone found my empty grave. So many years have passed all my friends and family are long gone. I am alone to wonder the world forever. My endless forever night.

Happiness was something from the past. A

feeling I have long forgotten. Feelings what are feelings? I have none. I have no heart. I have no idea what it is like to love someone. Or the feeling of someone loving me. *Am nothing but an empty shell that looks like a man in an animals clothing. God why do you hate me so much?*

Authors note.

To all my readers. I know this was a short story but the moral of it is God forgives everyone. All you need to do is ask him. And remember you are never alone. No matter of how bad of a life you have, anybody can change if they want to.

C. E. Metcalf

Made in the USA
Columbia, SC
17 October 2023

24200509R00019